WANTED:
Warm, Furry Friend

Macmillan Publishing Company,
866 Third Avenue, New York, NY 10022.
Collier Macmillan Canada, Inc.
Printed and bound in Hong Kong   First American Edition
10 9 8 7 6 5 4 3 2 1
The text of this book is set in 15 point ITC Newtext Light.
The illustrations are rendered in pen-and-ink and watercolor.
Library of Congress Cataloging-in-Publication Data
Calmenson, Stephanie. Wanted — warm, furry friend /
by Stephanie Calmenson; pictures by Amy Schwartz.
— 1st American ed.   p.   cm.
Summary: Two rabbits begin a satisfying correspondence,
unaware that they already know and dislike each other.
ISBN 0-02-716390-3
[1. Pen pals — Fiction. 2. Rabbits — Fiction.]
I. Schwartz, Amy, ill. II. Title.
PZ7.C136Wan 1990 [E] — dc19 88-13405 CIP AC

WANTED:
Warm, Furry Friend

BY

Stephanie Calmenson

PICTURES
BY

Amy Schwartz

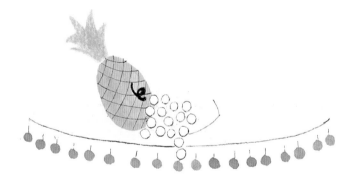

Macmillan Publishing Company
New York
Collier Macmillan Publishers
London

76936

Ralph was shopping for his dinner when he saw Alice walking down aisle three.

"Look at that strange hat," he thought. "That is one silly rabbit!"

Meantime, Alice had spotted Ralph. "Look at that shopping cart," she thought. "Carrots, carrots, and more carrots. That must be one boring rabbit!"

Alice and Ralph reached the check-out counter at the exact same moment. *Kaboom!* Their carts smashed together.

"So sorry," said Alice, not really meaning it.

"Quite all right," said Ralph, heading for another line.

Ralph and Alice did not know why they felt the way they did about each other. After all, they had never really spoken. They had just looked at each other one day and made up their minds not to get along.

That night, after eating a dinner of home-cooked carrots, Ralph sat down to read his newspaper. An ad opposite the sports page caught his eye. It said:

WANTED:
Warm, Furry Friend

I am a pretty and kindhearted rabbit looking for a friend. If you are looking for a friend, too, please write to me at Box 9, Woodland Station. I promise to write back.

"I could use a new friend," thought Ralph. "I spend too much time by myself."

Ralph sat back and thought about how he would answer. Then he took a pencil and paper from his drawer and wrote this letter:

Dear Box 9,

I was reading about the game between the Woodbashers and the Forest Cubs (Go, Bashers!) when I saw your ad. As a matter of fact, I have been looking for a kindhearted friend, but haven't met any lately. So maybe you and I could be friends.

Here are some things I like:

1. The Woodbashers!
2. Fishing
3. Rock and roll
4. Telling jokes (Here is one of my favorites: Why did the rabbit wear red suspenders?)

Your new friend

(I hope)

The next day when Ralph went to
mail his letter, he saw Alice.

"Look at those weird sneakers,"
thought Alice. "There's no doubt about
it. The rabbit is ridiculous!"

"I can't believe the way she walks,"
thought Ralph. "If I didn't know better,
I'd think she was a duck!"

Ralph tried to slip past Alice. Alice tried to slip past Ralph. But they went the same way and ended up tripping one another.

"So sorry," said Ralph.

"Quite all right," said Alice.

Over the next few weeks, Ralph wrote many letters to his new friend at Box 9. And he received many sweet letters in return.

She liked to dance and swim. Ralph did, too. She was a good cook and promised to invite him to dinner. In return, Ralph, who was an excellent carpenter, promised to fix her roof. And best of all, she knew that rabbits wear red suspenders to keep their pants up!

Ralph read over the letters each night, then gathered them in a bundle and tucked them under his pillow. He would want to meet his new friend soon. But for now he was happy just to dream of her.

One morning, Ralph decided to go out early to catch some fish for breakfast. When he arrived at his favorite spot, he ran into you-know-who.

Ralph and Alice sat as far away from each other as they could. But it wasn't far enough. When Alice tried to pull in a fish, their lines got all tangled together. Ralph tried to get them untangled, but that only made things worse. Soon Ralph and Alice were tied up in knots.

"So sorry," said Ralph.

"Quite all right," said Alice through clenched teeth.

By the time they were free again, Ralph and Alice were too tired to fish anymore and stomped off hungry and empty-handed.

"I'm glad I don't have to be friends with *that* rabbit," muttered Ralph.

Alice called back, "I don't want to
be your friend, anyway. There are other
rabbits in the woods, you know!"

"There sure are!" said Ralph. And he
hurried home to write to Box 9. This
time, he suggested they meet.

The date was set for Wednesday afternoon at three o'clock at Pop's Soda Shop. They each would bring a rose so they could recognize one another.

At two-thirty on Wednesday, Ralph set out for Pop's. As he was crossing the street, he got a glimpse of Alice waiting at the bus stop. He decided to let her get on the first bus and he would get on the one that followed. This was no time for trouble with some noodle-headed rabbit.

The next bus took a long time to come. It was almost three-thirty by the time Ralph got to Pop's. "I hope she hasn't left already," Ralph said to himself.

He peeked into Pop's window, eager
to see the sweet and charming rabbit
he had come to like so much.

"She did wait!" Ralph said, seeing
a rose in a glass on the table and a
sweater hanging from the chair. "She
must have gone to powder her nose."

Ralph went in and added his rose
to the glass. He tucked in his shirt and
then, noticing his shoelaces were open,
bent down to tie them.

Meantime, Alice was indeed powder-
ing her nose in the bathroom. "I hope he
hasn't forgotten," she said to herself.

When Alice got back to her table,
she was excited to see another rose
in the glass.

"He must have gone to fix his tie,"
she thought, not knowing that Ralph
was right there under the table, tying
his shoes.

Ralph finally sat up. "*You!!!!!!!!*" Ralph and Alice shouted together.
They raced for the door.

Ralph and Alice had been stuck in the doorway for quite some time when Alice asked, "Are you really the rabbit who likes to bunny hop till dawn?"

"Yes, I am," said Ralph. "And are you really the rabbit who knows the words to 'Bebop Bunny' by heart?"

"Yes," said Alice. "You know, I liked your jokes. They made me laugh."

"I liked yours, too," said Ralph. "Did you hear the one about the rabbit with the shiny nose?"

"You mean the one who wore her powder puff at the wrong end?" said Alice.

"That's the one!" said Ralph.

Ralph and Alice told each other more jokes. Then they remembered they were stuck in the doorway. That made them laugh so hard, they popped right out.

Ralph and Alice spent the rest of the afternoon together.

The next day, Alice cooked dinner for Ralph, while he fixed her roof.

They talked about all kinds of things and found out they really did like each other very much.

Eventually, Ralph and Alice married.

They had a beautiful wedding. Alice wore her favorite hat. And Ralph made sure the guests had plenty of carrots to eat.

It all worked out fine, because when you like someone, things like carrots and hats hardly matter at all.

While they were dancing, Ralph whispered in Alice's ear, "What do rabbits have that no other animals have?"

Of course Alice knew the answer....

"Baby rabbits!"

And when their children asked how
they met, Ralph and Alice told them the
whole story.